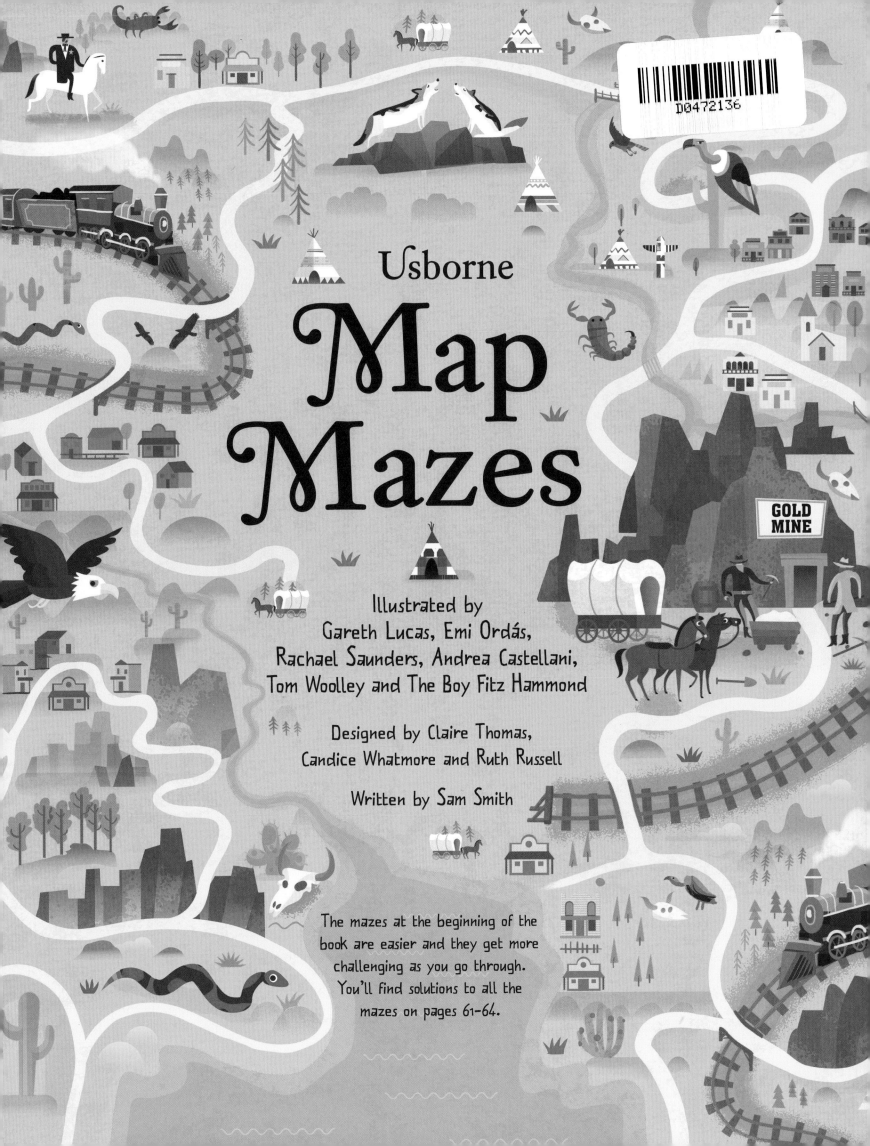

Usborne
Map Mazes

Illustrated by
Gareth Lucas, Emi Ordás,
Rachael Saunders, Andrea Castellani,
Tom Woolley and The Boy Fitz Hammond

Designed by Claire Thomas,
Candice Whatmore and Ruth Russell

Written by Sam Smith

GOLD MINE

The mazes at the beginning of the
book are easier and they get more
challenging as you go through.
You'll find solutions to all the
mazes on pages 61-64.

Visiting Valencia

"Motorcycle" Mike is cruising to Valencia for some fresh oranges and flamenco. Map a route for him across Europe, keeping to the dotted trails.

Tulips

Rheinturm Tower

The Crooked Forest

NETHERLANDS

Brandenburg Gate

GERMANY

Windmill

Bratwurst sausage and pretzel bread

Prague astronomical clock

POL

BELGIUM

CZECH REPUBL

LUXEMBOURG

Grapes

Traditional Austrian clothin

Eiffel Tower

FRANCE

Swiss chocolate

Neuschwanstein Castle

AUSTRIA

"Motorcycle" Mike

Camembert cheese

Tour de France

SWITZERLAND

The Alps

Canals of Venice

SLOVENIA

Croatian guard

Lascaux cave paintings

Milan fashion

CROATIA

Sunflowers

Lavender

Orange tile roofs of Dubrovnik

BOSNI HERZ

Sagrada Família church

ITALY

SPAIN

Leaning Tower of Pisa

Roman Colosseum

Valencia oranges

VALENCIA, SPAIN

Olives

Mount Etna

Flamenco dancer

2

Turkish travel

Find a route across town so the horse-drawn carriage can pick up some passengers outside the gold-domed mosque.

START

FINISH

Polar explorers

The captain's compass won't work properly at the Pole, and he's lost his way. Can you map out a clear route between the ice floes so his ship, the *Snow Goose*, can reach Base Camp?

Base Camp

5

Unicycle circus

Use the map below to lead Mr. Jelly through the grounds to the Big Top. He can't ride his unicycle over grass or along cobbled paths in case it makes him fall off.

FEATURING *Ringmaster Raymond*

CAROUSEL

SPIRAL SPECTACULAR

STRONG MAN

SHOOTING GALLERY

BIG WHEEL

BIG TOP

MYSTIC MOG

COCONUT CRASH

WELCOME

Cobbles look like this.

TEST YOUR STRENGTH

Mr. Jelly

Downtown drive

Find the red taxi a route through this bustling city to the green houseboat that's moored by the riverbank.

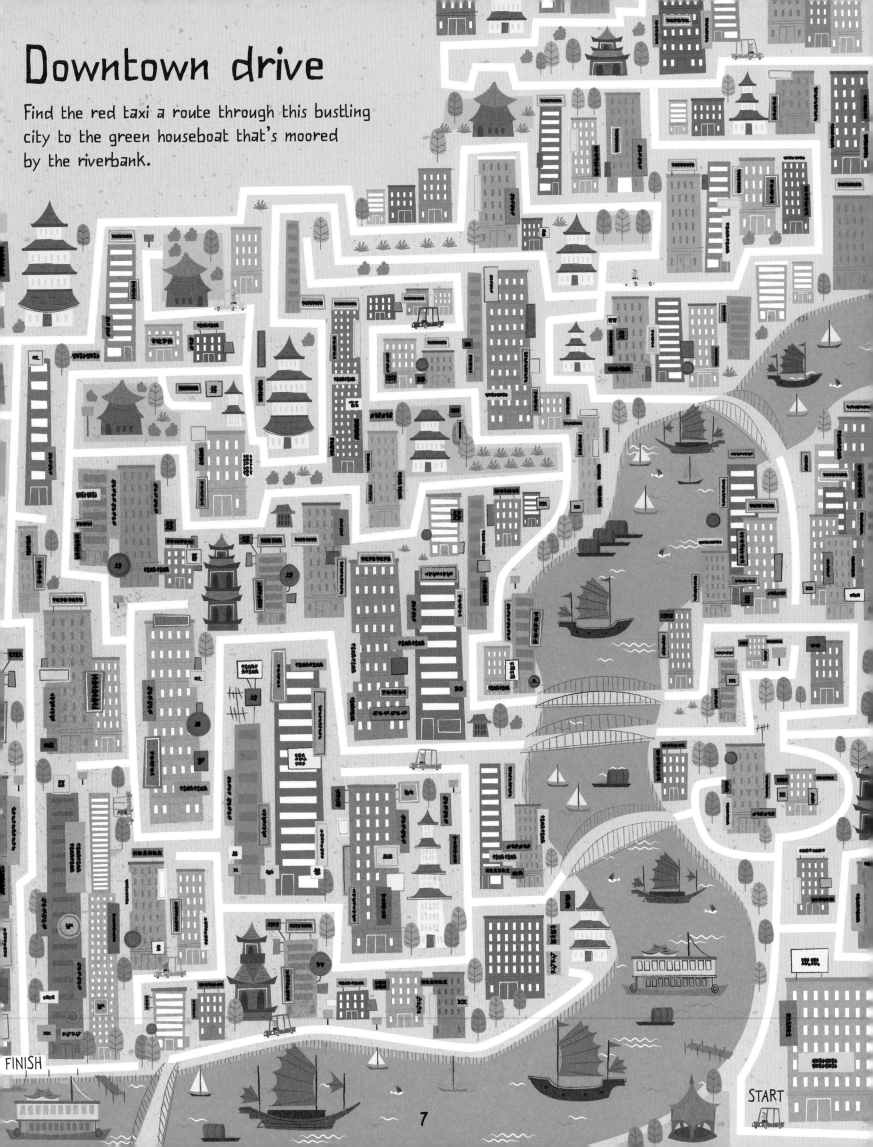

FINISH

START

The lost city

Intrepid explorer Penny Fawcett has discovered a map to the ancient lost city of Zacapasca. Help her find her way along the wall-top paths to reach the city's stepped pyramids buried deep in the jungle.

Penny Fawcett

Three Window Ruins

Temple of the Moon

Temple of the Dead

Temple of the Sea

DOLPHIN BAY

ALLIGATOR COAST

One way, Jose

Help Jose take the shortest route across town to his family waiting for him on the roof. He must obey the one-way system shown by the arrows.

Jose

FINISH

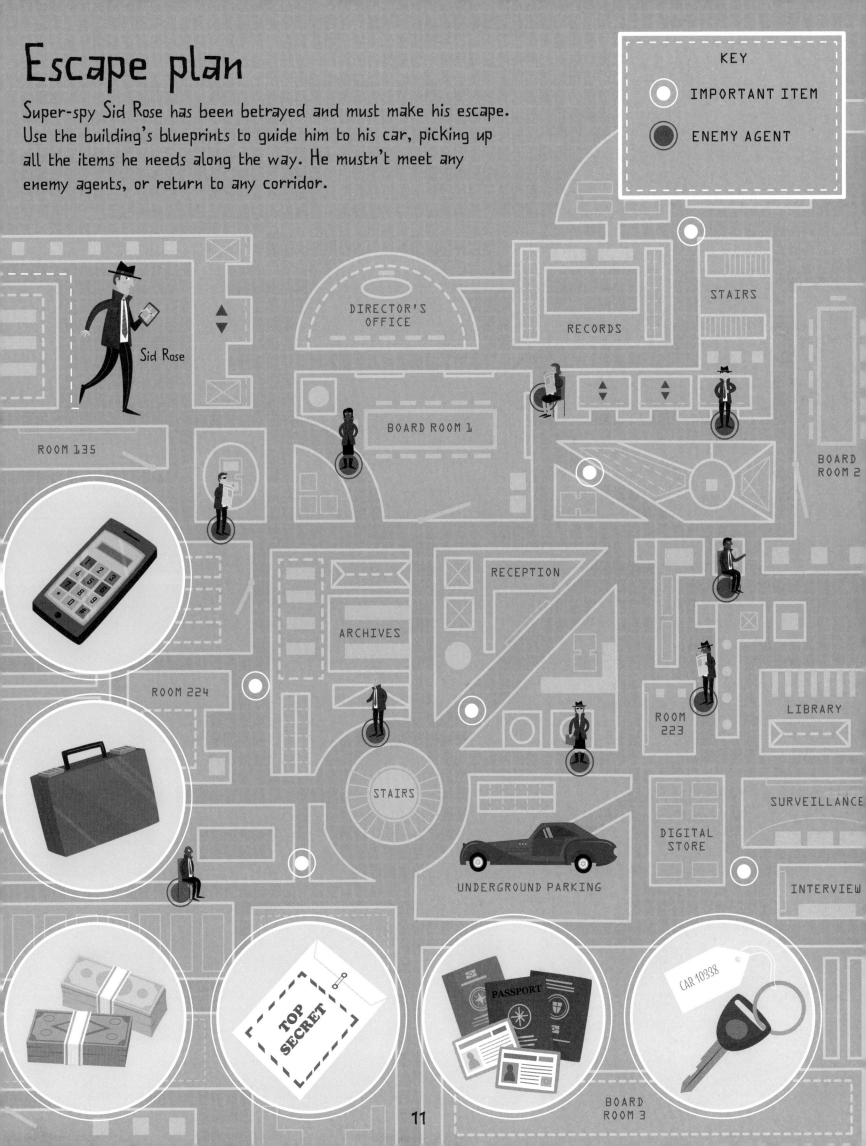

Escape plan

Super-spy Sid Rose has been betrayed and must make his escape. Use the building's blueprints to guide him to his car, picking up all the items he needs along the way. He mustn't meet any enemy agents, or return to any corridor.

KEY

○ IMPORTANT ITEM

● ENEMY AGENT

Sid Rose

ROOM 135

DIRECTOR'S OFFICE

RECORDS

STAIRS

BOARD ROOM 1

BOARD ROOM 2

RECEPTION

ARCHIVES

ROOM 224

LIBRARY

ROOM 223

STAIRS

SURVEILLANCE

DIGITAL STORE

INTERVIEW

UNDERGROUND PARKING

CAR 10338

TOP SECRET

PASSPORT

BOARD ROOM 3

11

Plundering pirates

The captain of the *Hungry Heron* has heard tales of remarkable riches buried on Treasure Island. Map a course along the sea chart's lines, so he and his crew can claim the legendary loot.

Monkey Island

Skull Island

Devil's Reef

Shipwreck Rocks

Mermaid Falls

Hungry Heron

Serpent Seas

Fire Island

Treasure
Island

Ghostly Galleon

Windmill Bay

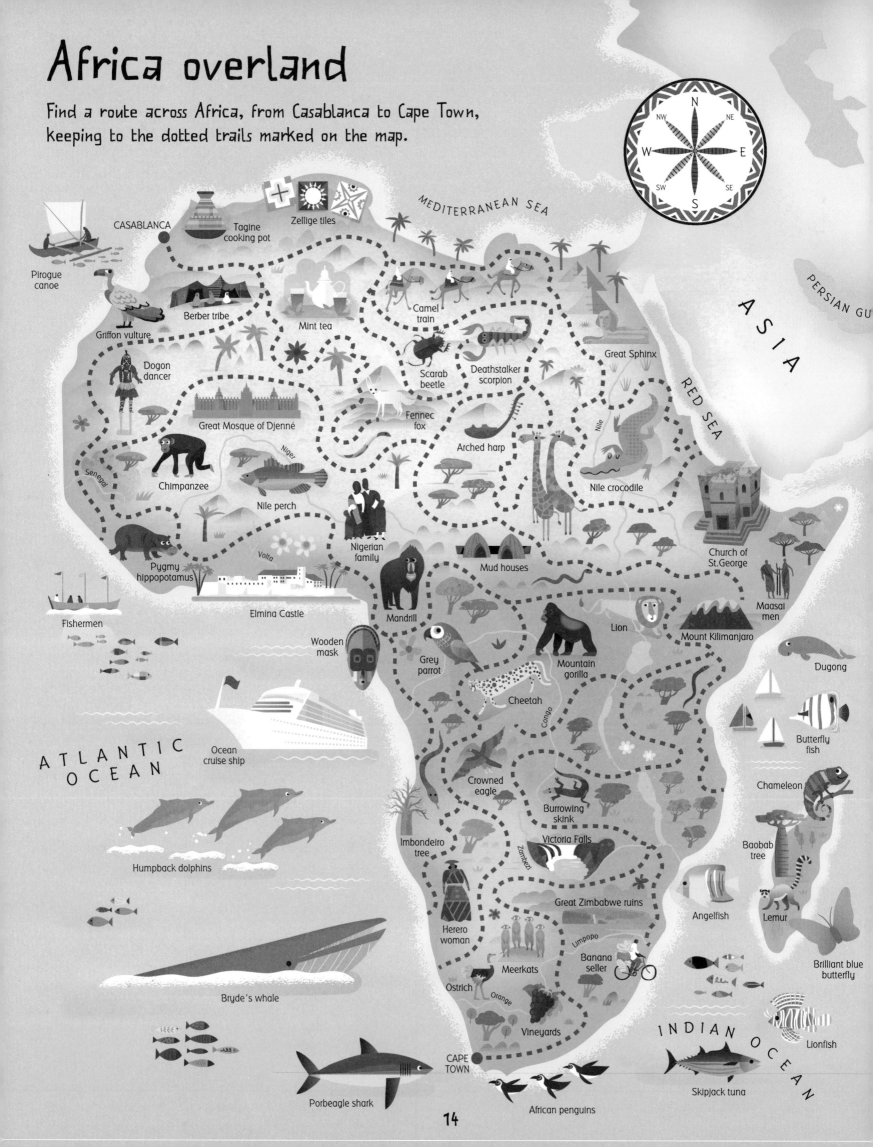

Alpine ascent

A group of hikers is staying at the Lakeside Lodge. Map a route for them through the mountains, keeping to the Alpine paths, so they can climb to the highest peak.

FINISH

Lakeside Lodge

London Olympics

It's 2012 and Veronica has a ticket to see the London Olympics. Plan her cycle route to the stadium, avoiding the busy roads marked with buses and taxis.

Veronica

LONDON ZOO

NELSON'S COLUMN

ST. PAUL'S CATHEDRAL

KENSINGTON PALACE

BIG BEN

HOUSES OF PARLIAMENT

LONDON EYE

NATURAL HISTORY MUSEUM

MI6 BUILDING

OLYMPIC STADIUM

TOWER OF
LONDON

THE GHERKIN

CANARY
WHARF

TOWER BRIDGE

Kelador quest

Sir Mark has been called upon for help by the mysterious maiden of Midnight Castle. Map a route across Kelador's wild woods and mighty mountains so he can complete his quest.

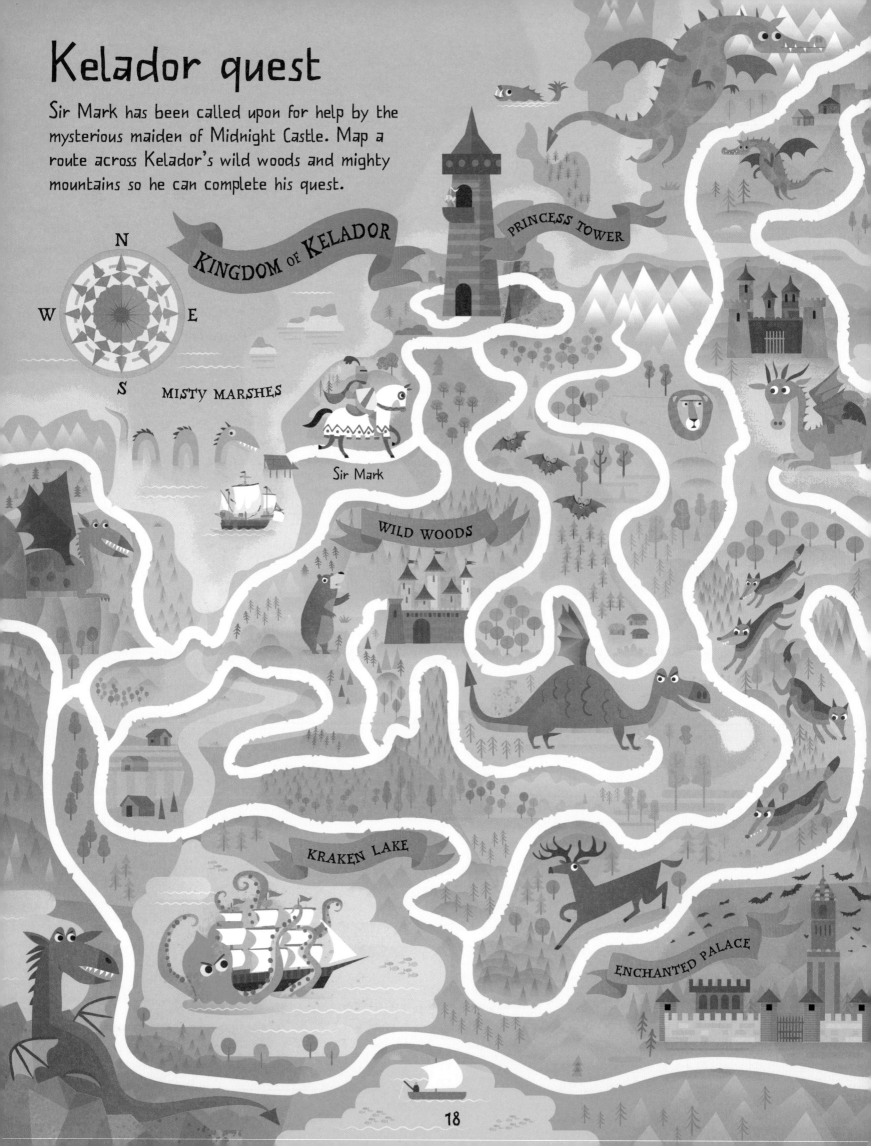

KINGDOM OF KELADOR

PRINCESS TOWER

MISTY MARSHES

Sir Mark

WILD WOODS

KRAKEN LAKE

ENCHANTED PALACE

CURSED TOWN

DRAGON'S LAIR

STAGNANT SWAMP

MIDNIGHT CASTLE

FORBIDDEN FRUIT

GIANTS' GORGE

CASTLE ENTRANCE

Museum map

This Natural History Museum has provided you with a handy map. Look at the layout, then plan a route around the exhibits so you only need to visit each room once.

ENTRANCE

EXIT

Country lanes

Find your way along the winding lanes to Cherry Cottage, starting at the signpost between Bramble Lane and Oakfield Road.

The Pastures

Furlong Road

Oakfield Road

Dovecote Way

Stables Street

Cornfields Road

Farmer's Way

Wheaten Lane

Mill Lane

Bramble Lane

The Pumpkin Patches

Cow Corner

Crop Corner

Plough Way

Grower's Green

Cherry Cottage

Primrose Lane

Barley Road

The Cottages

New Grove

Ben's Barn

Millstone End

Pony Drive

Buttercup Way

Hay Mile Road

Ewe Lane

Corn Corner

Herder's Way

Hogget Lane

Maize Road

Valley Farm

The Paddocks

Fir Lane

Stone House

Drover's Way

The Dell

Forest Green

Meadow Way

Milker's Road

Old Goat Road

Bridge Lane

Well Street

Seedling Street

Bridge Lane

The Oaks

The Old Well

Hay Mile Road

The Hedges

Orchard Road

Well Street

The Orchards

The Meadows

Beech End Road

Old Ox Way

Island getaway

The morning ferry has just dropped off its passengers in the old fishing village of Shingleton. Help them find their way from Dockers Lane to the Safe Haven Hotel, visiting Shingleton's famous fudge store along the way.

Seaview Gardens

Smugglers Lane

Halcyon Hill

Tidal Rise

Herring Lane

Scampi Square

Anglers Avenue

Curlew Street

Puffin Passage

Sailor's End

Neptune Way

The Crescent

Fudge

Cockle Row

Davy Jones Close

Shingle Avenue

Seahorse Road

Merchant Street

Shore Street

Whelk Walk

The Waterfront

Sandy Lane

Shingleton Beach

23

Hikers' retreat

The hikers are tired from their long trek through Bear Falls National Park, but they still have a little way to walk. Which trail should they take to pitch their tents for the night at Camp Cherokee?

CAMPSITES

HIKING TRAIL

CAMP CHINOOK

CAMP SIOUX

NAVAJO GORGE

LAKE WENATCHI

CAMP YAKAMA

24

CAMP PEQUOT

WISHRAM WATERFALL

FISHING SPOT

CAMP CHEROKEE

SALISH SOILS

Dog-walking duties

Diane the dog-walker has lots of canine clients today. Can you find her a route from Pug Place to Pedigree Park so she can collect all seven dogs on the way without going along any stretch of road twice?

NAME: Buster
BREED: Mixed

NAME: Dougie
BREED: Pug

NAME: Henry
BREED: Dachshund

NAME: Lady
BREED: Afghan

NAME: Titch
BREED: Mixed

NAME: Snappy
BREED: Chihuahua

NAME: Bouncer
BREED: Labrador

WETNOSE WOODS

Diane

Pug Place

Russell Road

Tail End

Kibble Street

Canis Corner

Corgi Close

Whippet Walk

Dalmatian Drive

Westie Way

Affenpinscher Avenue

Schnauzer Street

Snoopy Street

Whippet Walk

Bark Bridge

Alsatian Avenue

Collie Close

Mutt Mews

Lassie Lane

Poodle Row

Labrador Lane

Alsatian Avenue

Pooch Place

RIVER CHASE

Setter Street

Spaniel Way

Whippet Walk

Beagle Bridge

Airedale Avenue

Park Street

Toto Terrace

Terrier Terrace

Pongo Close

White Fang Way

Dachshund Drive

Park Road

Park Entrance

Retriever Road

Pointer Way

Lady Lane

King Charles Crescent

Saluki Str

Hound Hill

Retriever Road

Wolf Walk

PEDIGREE PARK

Fox Street

Bones Boulevard

Great Dane Lane

Slick Street

Growlers Grove

Mastiff Road

Waggers Walk

Perdita Way

Park Road

KENNEL COPSE

Saint Bernard Road

Gnasher's Knee

Staffie Street

Husky Hill

26

The pharaoh's tomb

Ernest the archaeologist has found a plan of a long-lost pharaoh's tomb. Can you find a way for Ernest to enter every relic-filled room just once and finish back where he started?

Ernest

New Year, New York

Lead Larry through the city to see the fireworks at Central Park. He must keep to the light-blue sidewalks and pedestrian crossings, but avoid the busy taxi stands marked by yellow taxis on the map.

One World Trade Center

Larry

Pedestrian crossings look like this.

Statue of Liberty

Empire State Building

New York Stock Exchange

Brooklyn Bridge

MADISON SQUARE GARDEN

NATURAL HISTORY MUSEUM

CENTRAL PARK

CHRYSLER BUILDING

GUGGENHEIM MUSEUM

Star City

The space pod must get to the T-10 Tower, but it's low on charge. Plan a route along the pink rails that goes to every power-up point on the map, without using any rail twice.

Power-up points look like this.

SHOPPING ZONE

THE MALL

START

FUN ZONE

HOTEL 360°

HOTEL 360°

PARK ZONE

9763

SPACE RADIO

i8 TOWER

T-10 TOWER

9760

FINISH

ROBOT GARAGE OPEN 24hrs

APARTMENT ZONE

Tour of India

Plan a route for a cycle race from Southern India to Ahmedabad, so it goes to each city on the map. The cyclists mustn't ride through any of the dark green tiger parks, or go anywhere twice.

New Delhi

Jaipur

Agra

Kolkata

Ahmedabad

Mumbai

Hyderabad

Arabian Sea

Chennai

Bangalore

Bay of Bengal

Kochi

START

Around the zoo

Rory wants to see the zoo's rare red pandas, but he's afraid of animals with wings. Plan him a path to the enclosure, and then to the exit, without entering bird or butterfly areas, or having to retrace his steps.

ON THE FARM

FLAMINGO LAKE

CHEEKY CHIMPANZEES

LEISURELY TORTOISES

ELEGANT OSTRICHES

MEERKAT MOUND

LAZY PANDAS

ANDEAN LLAMAS

ENTRANCE

Rory

RESTAURANT

LAID-BACK LEMURS

THE FOOD COURT

RED PANDAS

PENGUIN SPLASH

TROPICAL AQUARIUM

BUTTERFLY FARM

LOOKOUT POINT

REPTILE HOUSE

GIFT STORE

EXOTIC BIRDS

AFRICAN ZEBRAS

SLEEPY SLOTHS

EXIT

Sheriff showdown

The Bronco Brothers have broken into the Red Gorge gold mine. Which way should Sheriff Stanley ride to arrest them? He must not ride through any towns, or he could be ambushed by the rest of the gang.

DEAD MAN'S TOWN

EAST TOWN

WEST TOWN

LITTLE TOWN

RIVER TOWN

RANCH TOWN

Sheriff Stanley

LAKE TOWN

SILVER LAKE

OLD TOWN

BROOK TOWN

NEW TOWN

GOLD MINE

RIDGE TOWN

LITTLE LAKE

LAKE SERENE

MILL TOWN

Resort route

The Jacksons are just arriving at the Sandy Bay resort, but they're a little lost. Use the map to help them collect their keys from the reception building, then lead them to lodge five without retracing their route.

SANDY BAY

SEA VIEW PARKING

STEPS TO BEACH

SANDY BEACH

PICNIC AREA

CAMPING

TOILETS

4

5

6

SEA VIEW LODGES

FISHING LAKE

PLAY AREA

MINI GOLF

POOLSIDE LODGES

9

8

7

3

POOL

2

GREENSIDE LODGES

TOILETS

1

RECEPTION

PARKING

The Jacksons

LONG STAY PARKING

Water Wonderland

Plan a route around this water park to swim in each pool in the order on your ticket. You can only get in and out of pools using a slide or the steps, and you can't walk under the slides.

Steps look like this.

SPLASH!

START

TWISTY

Slip 'n' Slide

FUN FLUME

LOOPER

Slippydippy

SNACKS

FINISH

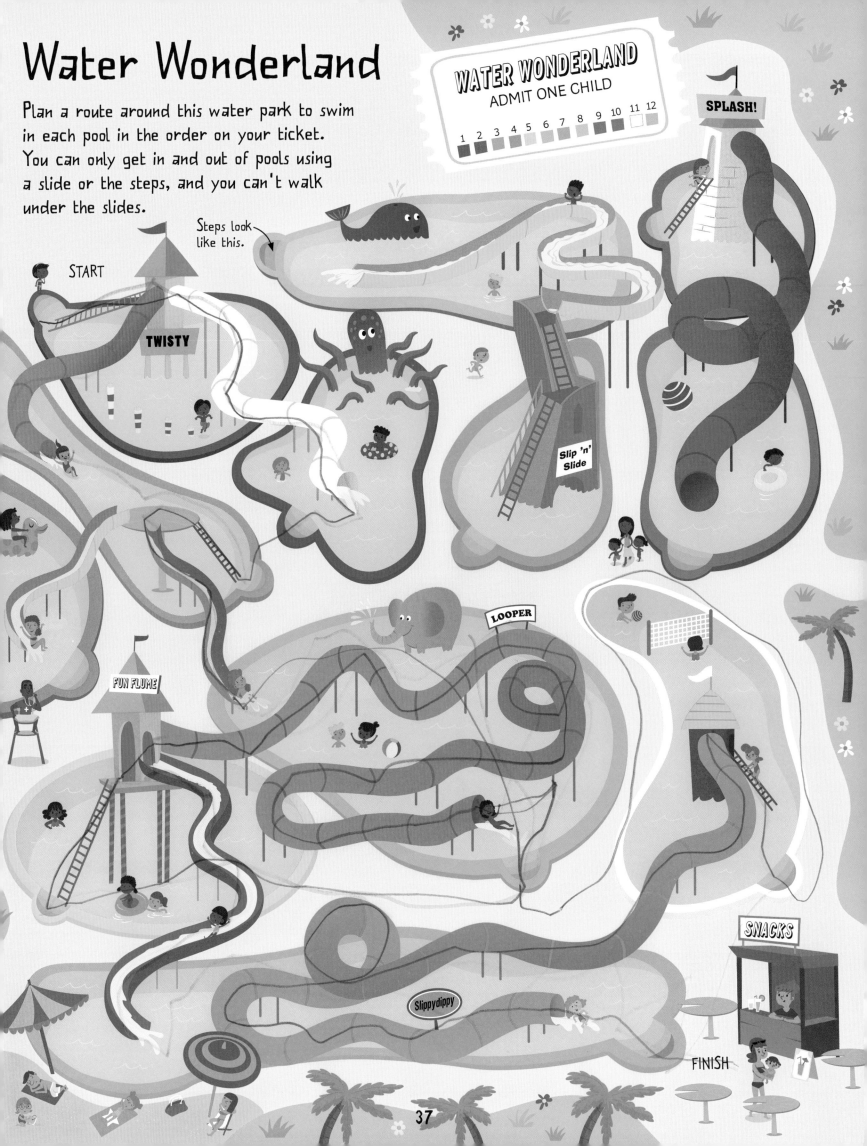

Underground round-trip

You're meeting friends for a picnic in the park, but first you need some food from the market. Starting and finishing at Piper's Gate, plan your route on the underground map so you don't go anywhere twice. (You can only change lines at circle stops.)

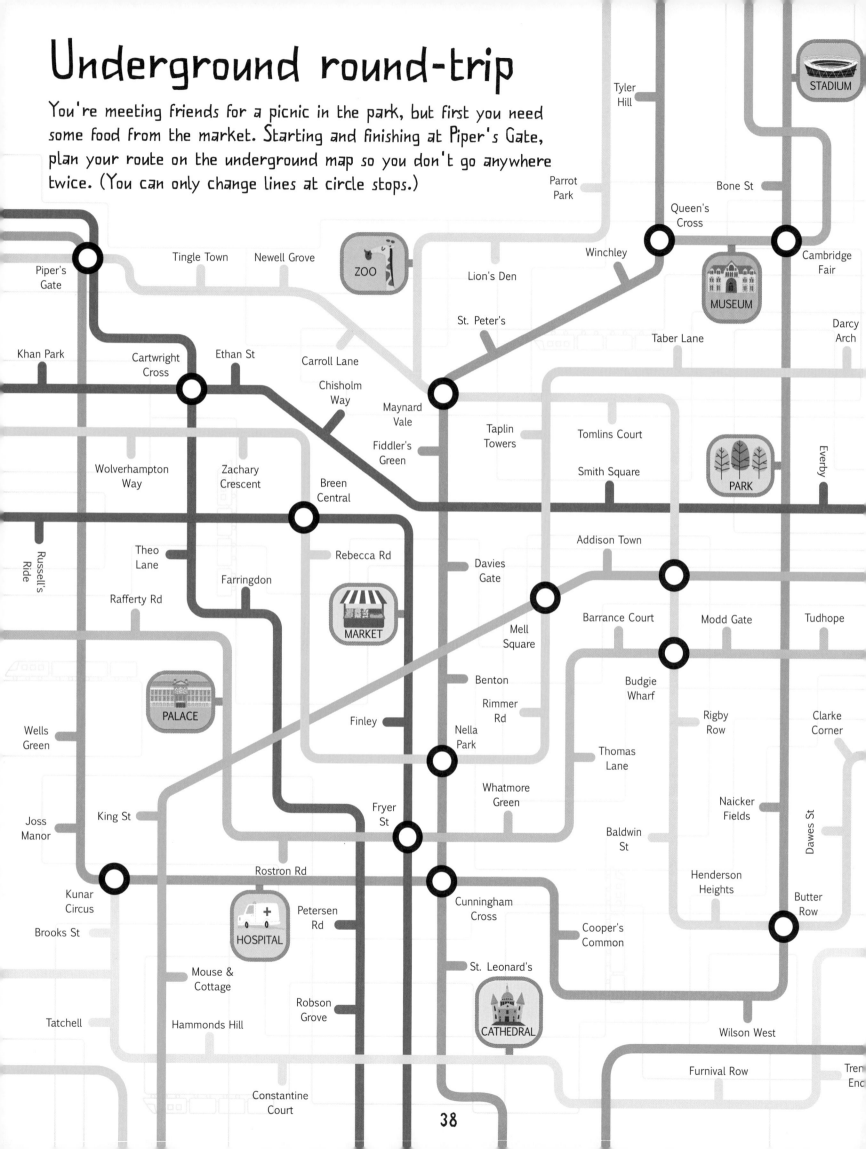

STADIUM

Tyler Hill

Parrot Park

Bone St

Queen's Cross

Winchley

ZOO

Lion's Den

Cambridge Fair

MUSEUM

Tingle Town

Newell Grove

St. Peter's

Taber Lane

Darcy Arch

Piper's Gate

Khan Park

Cartwright Cross

Ethan St

Carroll Lane

Chisholm Way

Maynard Vale

Taplin Towers

Tomlins Court

PARK

Everby

Fiddler's Green

Smith Square

Wolverhampton Way

Zachary Crescent

Breen Central

Addison Town

Russell's Ride

Theo Lane

Rebecca Rd

Davies Gate

Barrance Court

Modd Gate

Tudhope

Farringdon

Rafferty Rd

MARKET

Mell Square

Budgie Wharf

Rigby Row

Clarke Corner

Wells Green

PALACE

Benton

Rimmer Rd

Finley

Nella Park

Thomas Lane

Naicker Fields

Dawes St

Joss Manor

King St

Whatmore Green

Baldwin St

Fryer St

Rostron Rd

Cunningham Cross

Henderson Heights

Butter Row

Kunar Circus

HOSPITAL

Petersen Rd

Cooper's Common

Brooks St

Mouse & Cottage

St. Leonard's

Tatchell

Robson Grove

Hammonds Hill

CATHEDRAL

Wilson West

Furnival Row

Tren End

Constantine Court

38

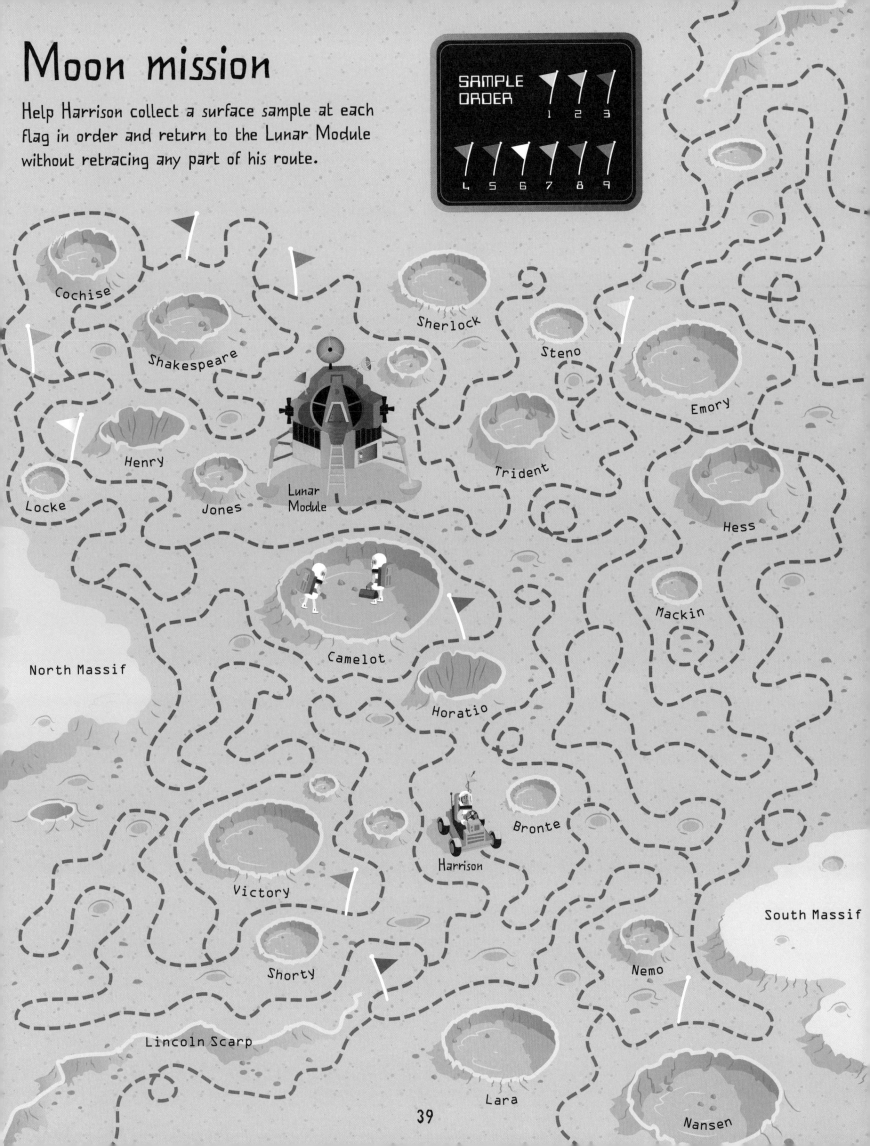

Moon mission

Help Harrison collect a surface sample at each flag in order and return to the Lunar Module without retracing any part of his route.

Detective disguise

Detective Godwin is undercover in this Victorian town, and must meet five informants at the places marked "i" on the map. How can he speak to each one on the way to his house on Richmond Road without retracing his steps or passing any policemen?

Detective Godwin

This is a policeman.

Highgrove Park

MARKET PLACE

Park Lane

Hampton Place

Wellington Place

Highgrove Place

SCHOOL LANE

Park Terrace

GEORGE STREET

HIGH STREET

OLD

David Street

Broadway Place

Church Place

ST. JUDE'S STREET

STREET

OLD STREET

Workhouse

Church

Church Street

Paddington Street

MILL STREET

Park Street Terrace

Park Street West

Queen's Terrace

PARK SQUARE

Brunswick Place

CRESCENT PARK

THE CRESCENT

Park Street East

Grove Park

Grove Lane

High Terrace

Green Terrace

HIGH STREET

Richmond Road

Detective Godwin's house

Richmond

The Informants

Miss Whipple

Samuel Brewer

Sir Seymour

Mrs. Cook

Jeffson

Trip down under

Find the route that lets the plane's passengers visit the most sites (27) before arriving at Queenstown. The pilot can only change paths at a site's red spot, and can't fly to any site twice.

START

Queenstown
New Zealand

Safari World

The tourists want to see all the Safari World wildlife on their way to Vista Village. Plan a path so their vehicle stops at every viewing point on the map, without taking any trail twice.

Viewing points look like this.

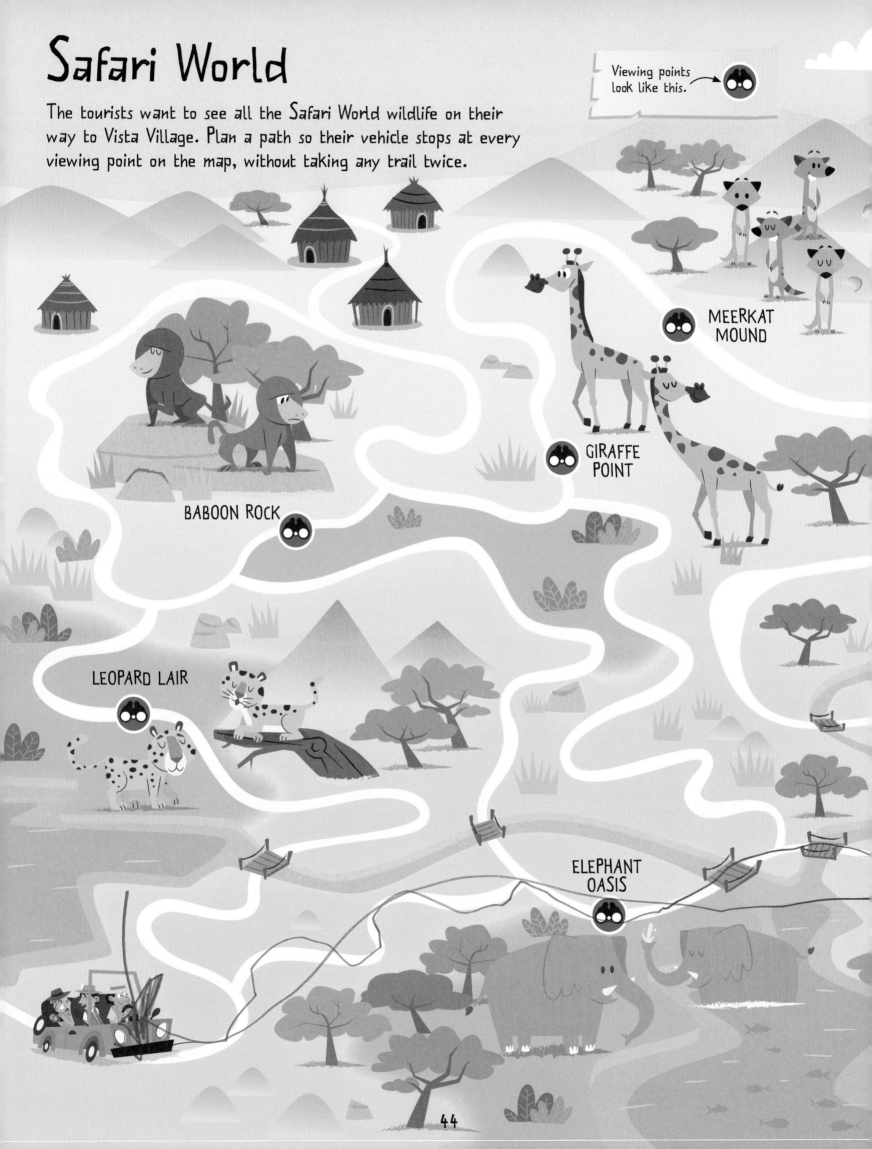

MEERKAT MOUND

GIRAFFE POINT

BABOON ROCK

LEOPARD LAIR

ELEPHANT OASIS

ZEBRA ZONE

HIPPO HOLLOW

FLAMINGO LAGOON

BIRD BASE

GAZELLE GRASSLANDS

VISTA VILLAGE

LION LOOKOUT

Ted's tulips

Ted has been collecting tulips from the fields and needs to return to his flower store to sell them. Show him the way back. (He can ride under bridges.)

TED'S STORE

Grand Canal

Ted

Ices of Venice

Pete is in Piazza San Marco and wants to try the ice cream at every store marked on the map on his way to Bellissima Gelateria. Which way should he walk through the Venice streets so he won't repeat any part of his route?

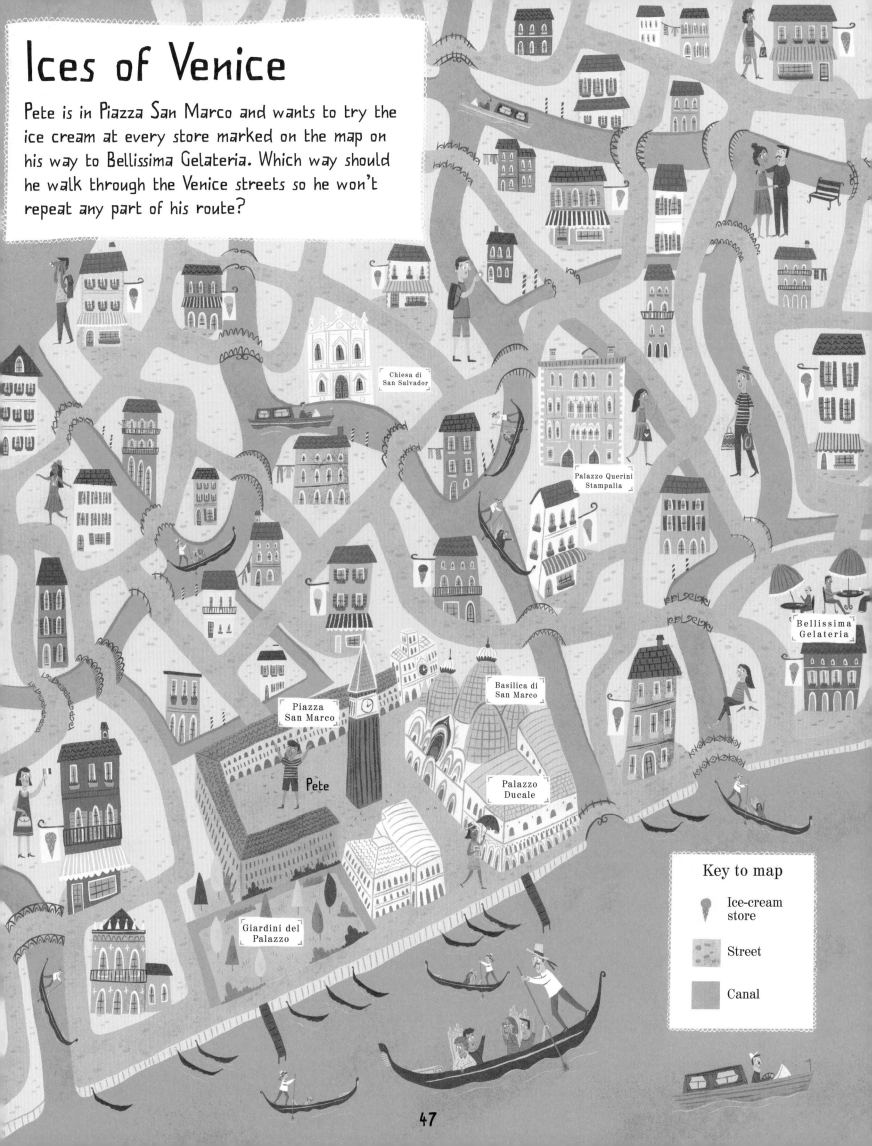

Chiesa di San Salvador

Palazzo Querini Stampalia

Bellissima Gelateria

Piazza San Marco

Basilica di San Marco

Pete

Palazzo Ducale

Giardini del Palazzo

Key to map

Ice-cream store

Street

Canal

Greenleaf Gardens

Plan a path from the manor house, through Greenleaf Gardens, to the play park, buying an ice-cream cone on your way. Don't open any of the gates or walk on the grass.

START

HEDGE MAZE

PLAY PARK

Ice cream

American road trip

Plan a road trip across North America, seeing all the things marked with red dots on your way to the White House, and without using any stretch of road twice.

MOOSE

LUMBERJACK

START

AMERICAN BISON

MOUNT RUSHMORE

REDWOOD TREES

BALD EAGLE

SHOW TIME

LAS VEGAS CASINOS

AMERICAN FOOTBALL PLAYER

GRAND CANYON

GOLDEN GATE BRIDGE

HOLLYWOOD

SONORAN DESERT

AMERICAN COWBOY

TEXAS OIL RIGS

ICE HOCKEY PLAYERS

CANADIAN MOUNTED POLICE

CANADA GEESE

MAPLE SYRUP

ICE FISHING

CN TOWER

WISCONSIN, AMERICA'S DAIRYLAND

INDIANAPOLIS MOTOR RACING

NIAGARA FALLS

CORN FIELDS

WHITE HOUSE

STATUE OF LIBERTY

BANJO PLAYER

JAZZ PLAYER

GEORGIA PEACHES

KENNEDY SPACE CENTER

STEAMBOAT

ALLIGATOR

N
NW NE
W E
SW SE
S

51

Bird spotting

Lizzie's listed the birds she'd like to see in South America. Start at the first sighting point, then trace a route along the trails so she can spot each bird in order. She can only change trails at sighting points, and she can't take the same trail twice.

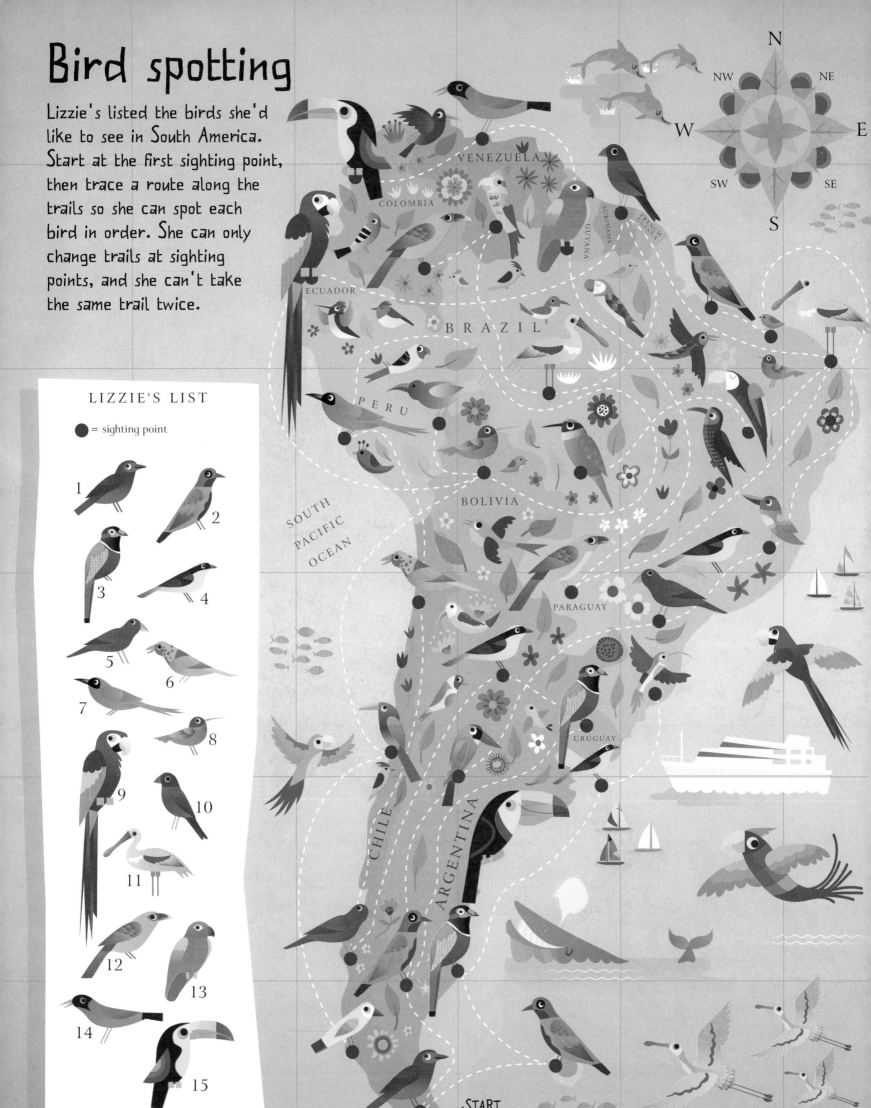

LIZZIE'S LIST

● = sighting point

1
2
3
4
5
6
7
8
9
10
11
12
13
14
15

START

Capital croissants

Delphine is determined to find the perfect Paris croissant.
Map out a route that takes her past every blue-roofed
bakery, finishing at the one on Rue Lecourbe.

Delphine

Avenue de Saint-Ouen

Sacré-Coeur

Arc de Triomphe

Champs-Élysées

Rue Royale

Eiffel Tower

River Seine

The Louvre

Boulevard Garibaldi

Rue Lecourbe

Notre-Dame

Luxembourg Palace

Boulevard Saint-Michel

N
W   E
S

53

Around the world

The hot-air balloon pilots are flying to Tokyo, but on their way they want to touch down at every destination with a yellow dot. Plan a route for them so they don't fly anywhere twice.

START

TOKYO, JAPAN

Cosmic quest

The alien astronaut has discovered a new galaxy. He has orders to explore all of its stars, but he's running low on fuel. Help the members of mission control guide him along the interstellar paths shown on their screen without taking him to any star twice.

Tropical cruise

Plot a course for the cruise ship to sail around these sunny islands. It must stop at every port marked on the map on its way to Costa del Tropicano, without going back on itself.

Costa del Tropicano

Ports look like this.

Palm Island

Dolphin Bay

Jungle Island

Monkey Island

Turtle Bay

Home-grown harvest

It's time to harvest some of your home-grown produce. Look at the layout of the growing areas, then plan a route to collect all the crops on the list below in that order. Use the marked entrances to go in each area, and don't go anywhere twice.

START

This is an entrance.

1. Apples
2. Cauliflower
3. Carrots
4. Radish
5. Raspberries
6. Tomatoes
7. Corn
8. Squash
9. Pumpkin
10. Cabbage

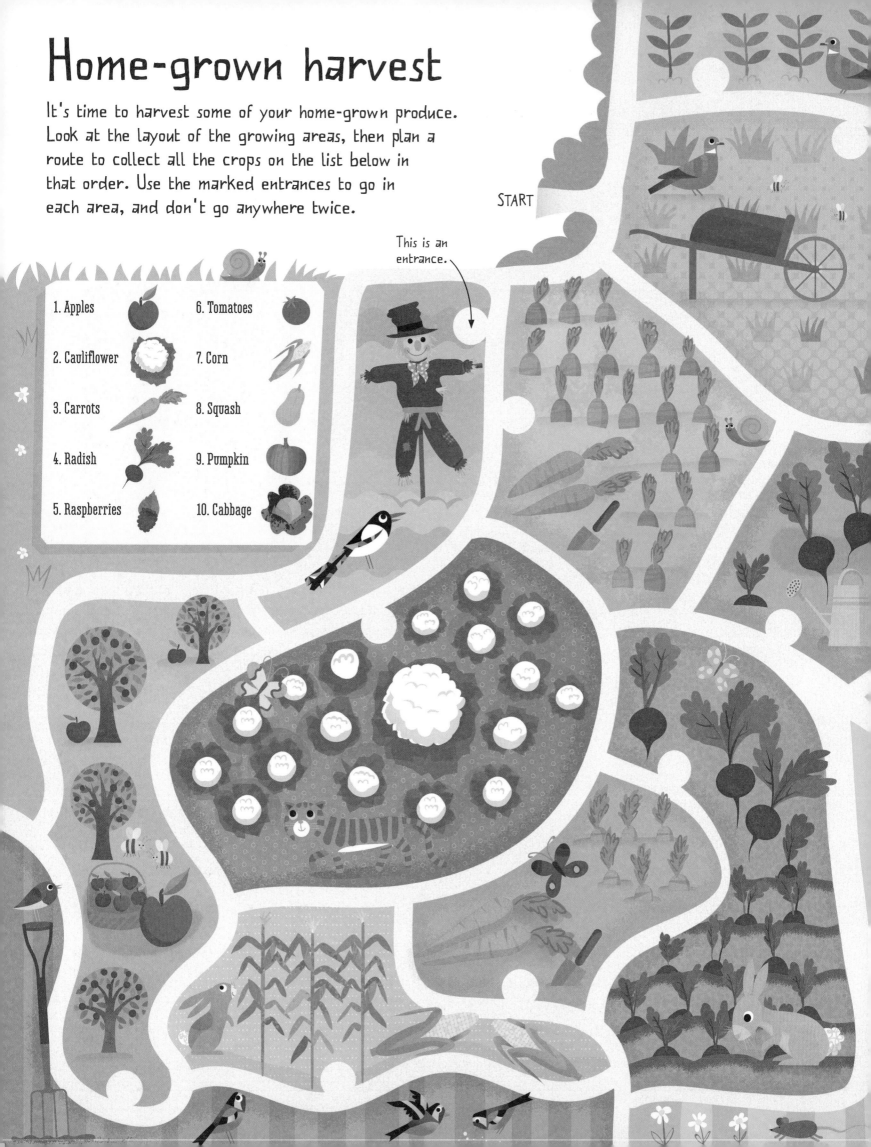

Finish

59

Whirlwind tour

Starting at Dover, plan a way around the UK and Ireland to see all the sights marked with a dot on the map. Don't retrace any part of your route, and visit London last.

London

Dover

2. Visiting Valencia

3. Turkish travel

4-5. Polar explorers

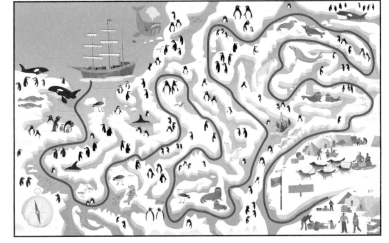

6. Unicycle circus

7. Downtown drive

8-9. The lost city

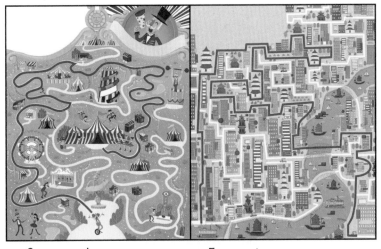

10. One way, Jose

11. Escape plan

12-13. Plundering pirates

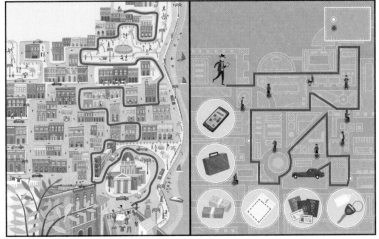

14. Africa overland

15. Alpine ascent

16-17. London Olympics

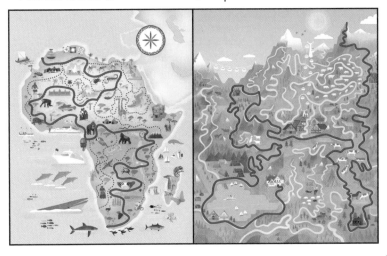

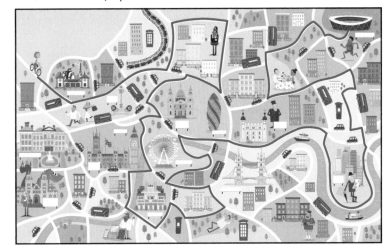

SOLUTIONS

18-19. Kelador quest

20. Museum map   21. Country lanes
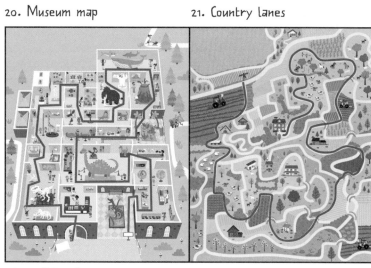

22-23. Island getaway

24-25. Hikers' retreat

26. Dog-walking duties   27. The pharaoh's tomb
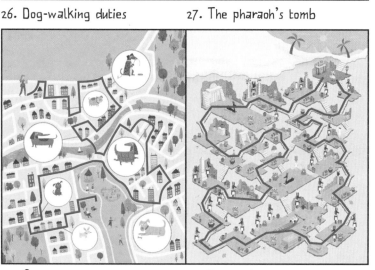

28-29. New Year, New York
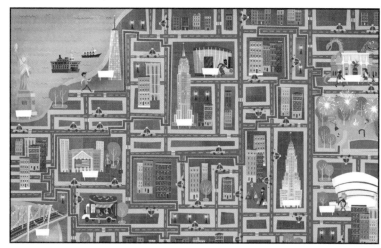

30. Star City   31. Tour of India
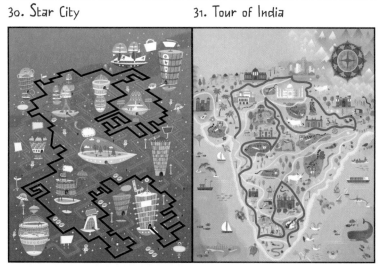

32-33. Around the zoo

34-35. Sheriff showdown

36. Resort route

37. Water Wonderland

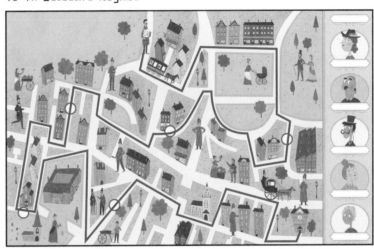

38. Underground round-trip

39. Moon mission

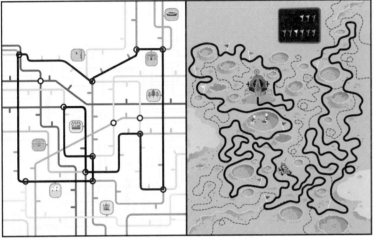

40-41. Detective disguise

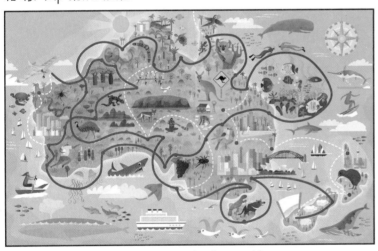

42-43. Trip down under

44-45. Safari World

46. Ted's tulips

47. Ices of Venice

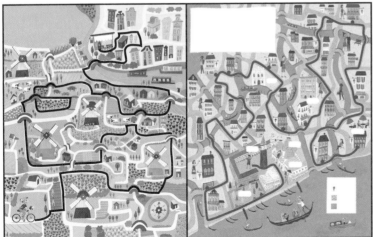

48-49. Greenleaf Gardens

50-51. American road trip

52. Bird spotting

53. Capital croissants

54-55. Around the world

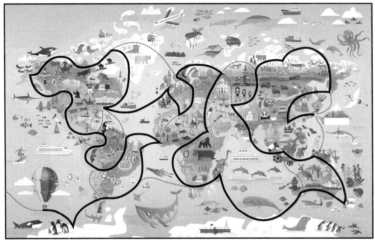

56. Cosmic quest

57. Tropical cruise

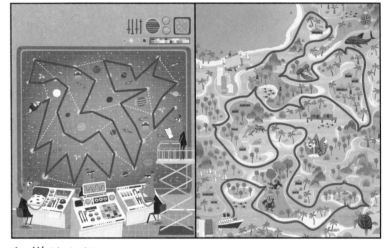

58-59. Home-grown harvest

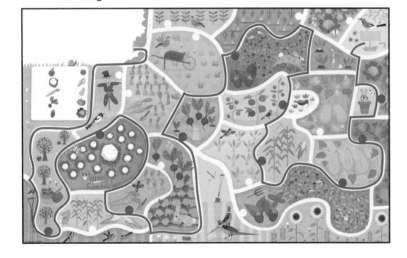

60. Whirlwind tour

Acknowledgements

Cover design by Jenny Addison

Additional illustrations by Mattia Cerato

Additional designs by Reuben Barrance and Laura Hammonds

Edited by Sam Taplin